P9-DDX-750

Teacher's Pets

Ready, Set, Dogs!

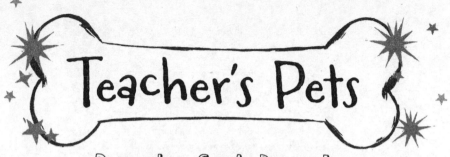

Teacher's Pets

Ready, Set, Dogs!

Stephanie Calmenson & Joanna Cole
illustrated by Heather Ross

SQUARE
FISH

Henry Holt and Company
New York

SQUARE
FISH

An Imprint of Macmillan
175 Fifth Avenue
New York, NY 10010
mackids.com

Library of Congress Cataloging-in-Publication Data
Calmenson, Stephanie, author.
Teacher's pets / Stephanie Calmenson and Joanna Cole ;
illustrated by Heather Ross.
pages   cm. — (Ready, set, dogs! ; 2)
Summary: "The girls are dismayed when their teacher is out sick and they have a substitute. Mr. Z
makes goofy jokes and can't keep the class under control. Worst of all, he doesn't say anything when
mean Darlene makes fun of Kate and Lucie. Luckily, once the girls turn into dogs, Kate and Lucie
learn they can save the day—and even make a new friend." —Provided by publisher
ISBN 978-0-8050-9647-7 (hardback)
ISBN 978-1-250-05705-1 (paperback)
ISBN 978-0-8050-9648-4 (e-book)
[1 . Dogs—Fiction. 2. Best friends—Fiction. 3. Friendship—Fiction.
4. Shapeshifting—Fiction. 5. Teachers—Fiction. 6. Schools—Fiction. 7. Humorous stories.]
I. Cole, Joanna, author. II. Ross, Heather, illustrator. III. Title.
PZ7 .C136Tc 2014   [Fic]—dc23   2014002031

Originally published in the United States by
Christy Ottaviano Books/Henry Holt and Company, LLC
First Square Fish Edition: 2015
Book designed by Ashley Halsey
Square Fish logo designed by Filomena Tuosto

10   9   8   7   6   5   4   3   2   1

AR: 3.3

To Mark
—S. C.

To Phil
—J. C.

Contents

Teacher's Pets

Ready, Set, Dogs!

Wake Up!

Crash! Bang! The sound of thunder came booming from Kate Farber's radio.

That got Kate up fast.

"Just kidding about the thunder," said Amos-on-the-Airwaves. "There's not a cloud in our beautiful Tuckertown sky."

Amos liked to keep his listeners laughing.

Kate grabbed her glasses from the night table and put them on. Her tan frames looked great with her dark brown hair and her freckles.

Then she grabbed her phone. It was right next to where her glasses had been. Kate was neat. She liked to know where her things were and lined them up in straight rows.

Kate was also a sensible girl. On school days, she made sure to call her best friend, Lucie Lopez. Without Kate's wake-up call, Lucie would be late every day.

Kate speed-dialed Lucie's number. She knew the special dog-bark ring that would be waking her friend. They both had the same ring. *Arfa-arf!*

Lucie and Kate loved dogs, and each wished she could have one. But they lived right next door to each other in garden apartments where the rule was NO DOGS ALLOWED.

So instead of real dogs, Kate and Lucie had sheets and pajamas with dogs on them. They had socks and underwear with dogs on them.

Kate had knickknack shelves with little glass dogs. Of course, they were lined up in neat rows.

Lucie had a collection of stuffed dogs scattered all over her room. Lucie was as messy as Kate was neat. She also had piles of dog books. She had read every single one, so she knew a lot about dogs.

Arfa-arf! Lucie's phone was ringing for the third time. Finally she picked up.

"Hullo," Lucie said, sounding half asleep. "What's up?"

"Obviously, not you," said Kate. "Hurry or we'll be late for school."

There was silence at the other end.

"Are you asleep again?" said Kate.

More silence.

"Wake up! Wake up!" said Kate.

"I'm up! I'm up!" said Lucie, almost falling out of her bed.

"See you outside."

Lucie and Kate had been friends since they were little, and they were in the same class at Tucker Elementary School.

They each got dressed.

Lucie put on her favorite pink poodle T-shirt. She loved pink. She also loved ribbons. She picked out a barrette that had curly pink ribbons hanging down. She pushed her ginger-colored bangs out of her eyes to admire the ribbons.

Kate didn't care much about ribbons. She put on her bulldog T-shirt. Then she quickly tied her hair in two perfect pigtails.

They didn't know it, but at the exact same time, both girls were putting on their pink dog-bone necklaces. They were the most amazing necklaces in the universe. Kate and Lucie wore them every day.

After breakfast, they met outside and

started on their way to school.

"Ms. Lu said we're going to do something fun today," said Lucie.

The girls couldn't wait to see what their teacher had planned. They walked a little faster. They came to the Lucky Find Thrift Shop just as Mrs. Bingly, the owner, was opening up.

"Hi, girls!" she called to Kate and Lucie.

"Woofa-woof!" they called back, touching their special necklaces.

They had bought them at Mrs. Bingly's store. Mrs. Bingly would never believe what those necklaces could do.

They had just passed the Lucky Find when Lucie started sniffing the air.

"Uh-oh," she said. "Do you smell what I smell?"

"You mean Banana-Fandana gum?" said Kate.

"Exactly," said Lucie. "And do you hear what I hear?"

Thunk, thunk, thunk.

"You mean that bouncing basketball?" said Kate.

"That would be it," said Lucie.

They turned and saw Danny DeMarco and DJ Jackson.

Danny had the basketball, but he had stopped bouncing it. Now he was holding it up in the air and spinning it on his finger. He was always doing something with that basketball.

And DJ was always chomping his Banana-Fandana gum. He usually chewed three pieces, but the girls had once seen him put four pieces in his mouth at the same time.

Sometimes Kate and Lucie had a good time with Danny and DJ, but most of the time, the girls thought they were the two most annoying boys on the planet.

"Hey, DJ," said Danny. "Do you see who I see?"

"You mean the two goofiest girls on the planet?" said DJ.

"Did he say girls?" whispered Kate, with a gleam in her eye.

"I believe he did," whispered Lucie.

"Woof?" said Kate.

"Woof!" said Lucie.

It was time to put their amazing dog-bone necklaces into action.

Chompy Chips

Kate and Lucie let Danny and DJ get ahead of them. Then they ducked behind a hedge where no one could see them.

The girls had discovered the magic of the necklaces by accident the day they found them at the Lucky Find Thrift Shop. Now they knew just what to do.

Kate and Lucie faced each other. At the exact same time, they said *"Woofa-woof!"* and gave each other high fives.

Woofa-wow! That did it! Their dog-bone

necklaces lit up. With a pop and a whoosh, Kate and Lucie weren't girls anymore. They were dogs!

No matter how many times it happened, they still couldn't believe it.

One dog was shaggy with ginger-colored fur that hung down almost to her eyes. The fur looked just like Lucie's bangs.

The other dog was white with tan spots, dark brown ears, and a brown patch around the eyes. The spots looked a lot like Kate's freckles. The dark brown ears were like her pigtails. And the patch around the eyes was like her glasses.

Instead of their necklaces, both dogs had silver collars with pink dog bones hanging down.

"We did it! We're dogs!" said Kate.

"It's showtime!" said Lucie.

They trotted out from behind the hedge,

wagging their tails. They ran to catch up with Danny and DJ, then danced back and forth ahead of them.

The boys had seen them around the neighborhood before.

"Hey, there are those cool dogs again," said Danny.

"Maybe we can get them to follow us to school," said DJ.

"Good idea," said Danny.

He turned to Kate and Lucie and said, "Dogs, follow!"

Instead of following, the dogs walked backward away from the boys.

"Wait! I know what to do!" said DJ.

He dug into his backpack and pulled out an open bag of Chompy Chips.

Boing! Kate's tail went up in the air. She loved Chompy Chips!

"Yoo-hoo, doggies!" DJ called, holding one out.

Shimmy-shimmy-shimmy! Lucie didn't wag just her tail. She wagged her whole behind. She loved Chompy Chips, too.

"Come and get it!" called Danny.

"Chompy Chips are so delicious," whispered Lucie.

Kate came to her senses fast.

"They are not delicious enough to make us go with those obnoxious boys," she whispered. "Follow me."

The dogs raced ahead of the boys and ducked behind the post office.

Without wasting a second, they barked *"Woofa-woof!"* as they tapped their paws together.

Woofa-wow! The dog bones on their collars

lit up, and Kate and Lucie were back to being girls.

"Do you think they'll give us any chips now?" said Kate.

"No way," said Lucie.

The boys came running. After they passed, the girls came out and caught up with them.

"Did you see two dogs?" said DJ.

"Dogs? What dogs?" said Kate.

"I don't see any dogs," said Lucie.

They rolled their eyes at Danny and DJ.

"Are you sure you know what dogs look like?" said Kate.

"Four legs? Furry? Waggy tails?" said Lucie.

Danny looked disgusted.

"It's no use talking to these goofy girls," he said, turning into the school yard.

DJ followed, stuffing the bag of chips back into his pack.

"We knew we wouldn't get any Chompy Chips," Lucie whispered.

DJ and Danny ran over to talk to some of their friends.

"We'll let you know if we see those dogs!" Kate called after them.

The girls linked arms and walked into school with their dog-bone necklaces twinkling in the sun.

Har-Har-Har!

Kate and Lucie were walking down the hall toward their classroom.

"Hi, Sara!" called Kate.

"Hi, Pete!" called Lucie.

Then they saw a long blond ponytail swishing up ahead. It belonged to a girl named Darleen.

"I hope she doesn't turn around," said Lucie.

"Me too. It's too early in the day for a Darleen-attack," said Kate.

Darleen made fun of Kate and Lucie because they were together so much. She liked saying, "Ooh, ooh, stuck like glue," and "Birds of a feather, always together."

Fortunately, Darleen decided to make a bathroom stop.

"That was close," said Kate, as they walked into their classroom.

They looked at the teacher and did a double take.

"Hey! That's not Ms. Lu," said Lucie.

"Unless she grew a mustache," said Pete, joking around as usual.

"And got a new hairdo," said Ben.

Julia walked in next.

"Ooh, a substitute!" she said.

"Please take your seats," said the teacher. "But don't take them far. Har-har-har." It was a wacky laugh that made the kids want to laugh, too.

In big letters he wrote his name on the board: MR. ZOLLICALAWAFFER.

"Zolli-cauliflower?" said Pete, with a big grin.

"Zolli-collie-wolly?" said Julia.

"Zolli-wolly-doodle all the day?" said Ben.

The kids were still trying to read the name when the teacher said, "Just call me Mr. Z."

"Thank goodness," said Kate.

Kate and Lucie sat down next to each other. Darleen slipped into her seat, which was right behind them.

"Ms. Lu has the flu," Mr. Z said. "Hey, Lu! Flu! It rhymes! Har-har-har!"

"Are you thinking what I'm thinking?" whispered Lucie.

"That we're going to have some fun today?" said Kate.

"Exactly," said Lucie.

Mr. Z cleared his throat. "Harrumph, har-rumph. Excuse me, I have a frog in my throat. And I believe there's an elephant in my ear. Har-har-har!"

"I've got a duck on my head," said Pete.

"You quack me up," said Mr. Z.

"Oh, great! Two class clowns," Lucie said to Kate. "And one's the teacher."

Mr. Z studied some papers on the desk.

"According to Ms. Lu's lesson plan, we'll be learning about animal communication," he said. "That's how animals tell each other things."

All at once, animal noises came from around the room. *Tweet! Meow! Hee-haw! Ribbit-ribbit!*

Kate and Lucie had to work hard to keep from barking.

"I love class participation," said Mr. Z.

"He might be sorry he said that," whispered Kate.

Mr. Z continued, "In addition to sounds, animals use body language."

"Uh-oh, here we go," said Lucie.

Two kids were already jumping like frogs. Another kid was flapping like a bird.

"I feel like wagging my tail," whispered Lucie. "Don't you?"

"At the moment, we don't have tails," Kate whispered back.

"Whisper, whisper," said Darleen. "You two sound like hissing snakes."

"Ugh. The first Darleen-attack of the day," Lucie said to Kate.

"Just ignore her," Kate said.

Meanwhile, the kids were getting wilder and wilder. In fact, they were out of control. But that didn't bother Mr. Z one bit. He talked right over them.

"For homework, please observe an animal communicating and be ready to tell about it," said Mr. Z.

The kids were still making animal noises. Mr. Z talked louder.

"There is also a class trip in your future," he called. "According to Ms. Lu, next week you'll be going to the zoo. Lu! Zoo! Another rhyme! Har-har-har!"

Mr. Z had to talk even louder than before. In fact, he was practically yelling.

"At the zoo, you'll be seeing some wild animals," he shouted.

"We're hearing some right now," said Pete.

"Yeah, it's a jungle in here," said Julia.

Growls, grunts, hoots, and howls filled the room.

Just then the bell rang, and the herd of wild animals went charging out the door.

Birds Peck, Cats Hiss

After school, Lucie and Kate stopped in at Mike's Mini-Mart. They had been thinking about Chompy Chips all day.

They each picked up a little bag. As they walked to the counter, a magazine about dogs caught their eye. It was called *Fetch It!* and had a droopy-eyed basset hound on the cover.

One of the headlines said "Chilly Dogs? Cozy Sweaters for Crisp Fall Days."

"I've got to read that," said Lucie, reaching for the magazine.

"No, you don't," said Kate, being sensible as usual. "We already have fur when we're dogs. And if our moms see dog sweaters in our closets, we're toast."

"Toasty warm," said Lucie. "In our cute new sweaters."

"Enough with the sweaters," said Kate, rolling her eyes.

"Maybe I'll knit one," said Lucie.

"There's no time for knitting. We have homework to do," said Kate.

"Oh, all right," said Lucie.

They paid for their chips and went to look for some examples of animal communication.

"The best way to observe animals is to be animals," said Kate.

"We'll get an A for sure," said Lucie. "Let's go!"

The girls went into the alley next to the mini-mart.

"Woofa-woof!" High fives!

With a pop and a whoosh, out walked two dogs.

The white, spotted one pranced quickly down the street.

The shaggy ginger-colored one stopped to sniff a fire hydrant.

"Hurry up!" said Kate. "Don't be so slow."

"Slow down," said Lucie. "Don't be so fast."

Kate slowed down. Lucie speeded up. And they kept going.

"Check out those pigeons," said Lucie.

"Okay, maybe we'll see some animal communication," said Kate.

Up ahead, a pigeon was pecking at a crust of bread. Another pigeon swooped down and landed nearby. It eyed the bread and stepped closer. The first pigeon pecked faster. The second pigeon went closer. Then the first pigeon fanned its tail. It clicked its beak. It leaped forward and pecked at the other bird. The second bird flew away.

"Fanning. Clicking. Pecking," said Lucie. "Excellent communication."

"Homework's done," said Kate.

"Let's go home," said Lucie.

The two dogs trotted up the street. They stopped to look at some store windows.

Up the block, Mrs. Patel was sweeping outside her clothing shop. The girl dogs wagged their tails.

Then they saw Tiger, Mrs. Patel's cat. They

loved Tiger. He had the softest orange fur. Lucie totally forgot about being a dog and went to pet him.

"Wait! What are you doing?" called Kate.

Uh-oh. Too late. When Tiger saw a dog coming at him, he really did turn into a tiger!

His ears went flat on his head, his back arched, his fur stood on end. He showed his teeth and hissed. Worst of all, out came his claws. Swat! Right across Lucie's nose.

"Ouch!" said Lucie.

"I tried to warn you," said Kate.

"I'll be okay," said Lucie. "And it was worth it. It was a great example of animal communication."

"Our homework's really done now," said Kate.

"And I have the nose to prove it," said Lucie.

Snip! Snip!

Before they got home, the dogs found a hiding spot and changed back into girls.

"Let's go to my house," said Kate.

When they walked in, Kate's mom was putting icing flowers on a pink layer cake. Her job was baking cookies, cakes, and pies that were sold at the farmers' market and at Didi's Bakery.

At the same time, she was talking on the phone.

"I bet I know who she's talking to," Kate said to Lucie.

"Of course. It's my mom," said Lucie.

"Hi, Moms!" the girls called together.

Mrs. Farber put the phone on speaker.

Lucie's mom was home from her job teaching at the Little Apple School House.

Their moms were best friends, just like they were. They were single parents who helped each other out a lot. They also talked on the phone a lot, just like Kate and Lucie.

"How did you get that scratch on your nose, Lucie?" asked Mrs. Farber.

"We met a cat in a bad mood," said Kate.

"You'd better go wash it and put on a Band-Aid," said Mrs. Lopez through the speaker.

"And would you please wash your hands, too?" said Kate's mom. "Remember, I'm allergic to cats."

Kate and Lucie went to do some first aid

and wash up. When they came back, their moms were still on the phone.

"Other than the cat, how was your day?" asked Lucie's mom.

"It was pretty wild," said Kate.

"So is your hair," said Kate's mom. "You must have been in a tornado."

"It's a good thing we're going to Fast Snips today," said Mrs. Lopez. "Lucie, your bangs have been getting so long, you look like a shaggy dog."

Kate and Lucie looked at each other and burst out laughing.

"It wasn't that funny," said Mrs. Lopez.

"If she only knew," whispered Lucie.

"Come on, girls, we'd better get going," said Mrs. Farber.

"I'll drive," said Mrs. Lopez.

They met outside and all four piled into the car.

"So, why was your day so wild?" asked Mrs. Lopez, as she pulled out of the driveway.

"Ms. Lu was out. We had a substitute," said Kate. "You should have seen him!"

"You should have heard him," said Lucie.

Together the girls said, "Har-har-har!"

"Was he nice?" said Kate's mom.

Kate stopped to think.

"You know, he was," she said.

"In a goofy kind of way," said Lucie.

They pulled into a parking spot right in front of Fast Snips.

Kate and Lucie couldn't believe who they saw. Darleen was walking out with a freshly trimmed ponytail.

As soon as she saw Kate and Lucie, she said, "Oh, puh-lease! You two even get your hair cut together?"

"Yes, aren't we lucky?" said Lucie.

"More like yucky," said Darleen.

"That was pretty snippy," whispered Kate to Lucie. "Get it? Snippy? Fast Snips?"

"Come on, girls, Millie and Muriel are waiting," said Kate's mom.

Kate and Lucie each took a seat in front of the big mirror.

"What have you done to your hair?" asked Muriel, as she tried to comb out Kate's knots.

"They were recently in a tornado," said Mrs. Farber.

"I can see that," said Millie, trying to undo Lucie's tangles.

Finally Millie and Muriel started cutting. *Snip, snip.*

"Eek! Don't cut my bangs too short," said Lucie.

"I haven't touched them yet," said Millie.

"Wait! Watch out for my ear," said Kate.

"I'm nowhere near it," said Muriel.

"Girls, please let Millie and Muriel do their job," said Mrs. Lopez.

"They've never given you a haircut you didn't like," said Mrs. Farber.

Snip, snip. The girls didn't say another word.

When their haircuts were finished, Kate and Lucie liked what they saw.

"Thanks, Muriel! Thanks, Millie!" they said.

Back in the car, the moms started whispering to each other. Kate and Lucie knew something was up.

"We'll be going to see Millie and Muriel ourselves," said Mrs. Farber.

"Yes, we have to look our best for Saturday lunch," said Mrs. Lopez.

"Why? Where are we going?" said Kate.

"You're not going anywhere. We are," said Mrs. Farber.

"That's right," said Mrs. Lopez. "We're going on a double date."

"Really?" said Lucie.

"Who are you going with?" said Kate.

"We don't know. It's a blind date. A friend set it up for us," said Mrs. Lopez.

"You mean you've never even seen the guys?" said Lucie.

"They could be goofy," said Kate.

"They could be like Danny and DJ!" said Lucie.

"Horrors!" said Kate.

"Now, girls, be nice," said Lucie's mom.

"You don't know Danny and DJ," said Kate. "They are extremely annoying!"

"Well, it's just one date," said Mrs. Lopez. "And it's not with Danny and DJ."

"Anyway, the two of us will be together," said Mrs. Farber. "So whatever happens, we'll have fun."

Lucie and Kate knew just what she meant.

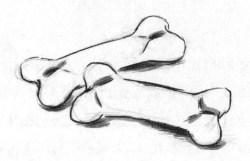

Hoots and Howls

The girls thought Ms. Lu would be back at school the next morning. But Mr. Z was there again. He said Ms. Lu would be back on Monday. The first lesson of the day was math. Then the class did some map reading for social studies.

When they finished social studies, Mr. Z reached under his desk.

"Can you read this?" he said, pulling out a big poster.

The poster had one word on it: THIS.

"Har-har-har," he laughed.

The kids started laughing, too.

Mr. Z reached for another poster. Before holding it up, he said, "We are now going to study advanced philosophical teleology."

Huh? The kids stopped laughing and gasped.

"Har-har-har again! Just kidding," said Mr. Z.

The poster he held up said WHAT DO YOU CALL A FISH THAT CHASES MICE?

"Who knows the answer?" asked Mr. Z.

"A shark!" called Ben.

"A mousetrap!" called Sara.

"A meanie-mo!" called Juan.

"Har-har-har! Good tries, but I didn't hear the answer I'm looking for," said Mr. Z. "Darleen, what do you call a fish that chases mice? Can you read the answer?"

He turned the poster over so Darleen could see the answer.

"A catfish!" read Darleen.

"Har-har-har!" laughed Mr. Z.

He shared three more funny posters, then said, "After lunch, we'll get back to studying animal communication."

A single tweet came from the back of the room. It was followed by a hee-haw.

"Uh-oh," said Kate.

"Here we go again," said Lucie.

In no time, the room was even noisier than the day before. There were the same meows, tweets, hee-haws, ribbits, growls, grunts, hoots, and howls. And now there were moos,

chitters, chatters, oinks, and cock-a-doodle-doos.

Darleen yelled, "Quack-quack!" right in Kate's and Lucie's ears.

Fortunately, the lunch bell rang.

"What a relief," said Kate.

"Let's go before the stampede," said Lucie.

In the lunchroom, Kate and Lucie each grabbed a tray.

Danny and DJ came up behind them.

"This food isn't fit for a dog," said Danny.

"I could use a liver snap myself," Lucie whispered to Kate.

"Guess what. We have a substitute," said Kate.

"We've got one, too," said DJ.

"Ours is wild," said Lucie.

"And funny," said Kate. "Har-har-har."

"Did you say, 'Har-har-har'?" said Danny.

"He sounds just like our sub," said DJ, as the boys walked off.

"They can't have the same sub," said Lucie when they left.

"It's not possible," said Kate.

"Unless Mr. Z is running back and forth," said Lucie. "Har-har-har."

Dancing Dogs

At the end of the day, the kids flew out into the school yard.

"All that animal talk was making me feel waggy," said Kate.

"Me too," said Lucie. "Woof?"

"Woof!" said Kate.

They waited till the school yard cleared. Then they ducked into the crawl tunnel in the playground area.

They turned to face each other, said "*Woofa-woof*," and gave high fives. The dog bones on their necklaces lit up. With a pop and a whoosh, two dogs came crawling out of the tunnel wearing silver collars with pink dog bones hanging down.

Just then, Mr. Z looked out the window. He couldn't believe his eyes.

Dogs? In the school yard? That's not allowed.

"No way. What a day," said Mr. Z to himself. "Way, day. That rhymes. Har-har-har."

He closed his eyes and shook his head to clear it. When he opened his eyes again, the dogs were gone.

Kate and Lucie had left the yard and were happily going up one street and down another.

Boing! All of a sudden, Kate's tail went straight up in the air, and she took off.

"Where are you going?" said Lucie.

"Squirrel alert! Squirrel alert!" called Kate.

"Leave those poor squirrels alone," said Lucie.

"I can't help it. It's in my blood!" said Kate.

Fortunately, it was in the squirrel's blood to be able to race up a tree to safety.

Kate slowed down, panting, and they kept going.

"It's fun having Mr. Z for a substitute," said Lucie. "But I miss Ms. Lu."

"Me too," said Kate. "We should buy her a get-well card."

"No. Let's make her one!" said Lucie.

"We can do it as soon as we're back to being girls," said Kate.

"What will we write?" said Lucie.

"Let's make up a poem," said Kate.

"How about 'Achoo! Ms. Lu!'?" said Lucie.

"That's a Ms. Lu rhyme. Mr. Z would love it!" said Kate.

"Har-har-har," said Lucie. "Let's keep going."

Between sniffing fire hydrants and barking at squirrels, the girls went back and forth till they had a poem they liked.

Achoo! Ms. Lu!
We're sad you have the flu.
Sneezing is no fun to do.
While you're at home, we're missing you.
Get well fast. Please do.
We want you back, Ms. Lu!

"We can put a heart on the card," said Lucie.

"And lots of sparkles," said Kate.

Suddenly, they both stopped. There was a mailbox with the name Lu on it. It was in front of a house with a big picture window.

"Omigosh, look who's there!" said Kate.

"It's our Ms. Lu," said Lucie. "She looks really sick."

Ms. Lu was stretched out on the couch. Her nose was red, and there was a box of tissues by her side. She sneezed.

"Just like in our poem!" said Lucie.

"Achoo! Ms. Lu!" the girls said together.

"She needs cheering up," said Lucie.

"And we are just the dogs to do it," said Kate.

They trotted onto the lawn and barked a couple of times to get Ms. Lu's attention.

"It's showtime!" said Lucie.

"Performers, take your places!" said Kate.

The dogs stood side by side in front of

the window. They got on their hind legs and waved their paws up and down. A big smile spread across Ms. Lu's face.

"Remember the dancing dogs we once saw at the circus?" said Kate.

"I do!" said Lucie. "Let's do it!"

They began to dance. Hop. Twirl. Dip. Roll over! Hop. Twirl. Dip. Roll over!

Ms. Lu started to laugh. That made her cough. And cough and cough.

"Uh-oh. I think we've cheered her up enough," said Lucie.

"Wait, we need a grand finale," said Kate.

They turned around and put their tails together to make a big heart. It was even better than a greeting card.

Ms. Lu began to clap. Kate and Lucie took their bows. Then they pranced off down the street, with the pink dog bones on their collars twinkling in the sun.

8

May We Be Excused?

Friday morning at school went surprisingly well. Kate and Lucie were settling in at their desks. Kate was lining up her pencil, sharpener, and eraser in a neat row.

Meanwhile Lucie was looking for a pencil. And looking. And looking. It was hard to find anything in her messy desk.

"Here, take one of mine," said Kate, rolling her eyes.

The morning lessons were spelling and math, and there were hardly any animal noises at all.

When the class came back after lunch, Mr. Z was standing at the door. He didn't say a word. He just waved at each kid.

After everyone had sat down, Mr. Z said, "What was I doing when you came in?"

"Shooing away a fly?" said Pete. "Bzzzz."

Everyone laughed.

"Har-har-har. Nice try," said Mr. Z. "I was using body language to say hello. What would I do if I were an elephant?"

The kids raised their arms in the air like trunks. Of course, they started trumpeting, too.

"Here we go again," said Kate.

"How would I say hello if I were a dog?" said Mr. Z.

"Now he's talking our language," Lucie whispered.

Some kids started barking.

Pete and Ben got up, turned around, and wagged hello with their behinds.

"Dogs say lots of things with their tails," Lucie called out. "Not just hello. Sometimes the tail says stay away."

"Sometimes it says I'm scared," said Kate.

"Tails are very talkative," said Lucie.

"How do you two know?" whispered Darleen. "I bet you don't even have dogs."

"Grrrr," Lucie growled under her breath.

"You're just know-it-alls," said Darleen.

Lucie and Kate looked at each other. Then Lucie wrote on a piece of paper: WOOF?

Kate read it and wrote back: WOOF!

She raised her hand and said, "May I please be excused?"

"Yes, you may," said Mr. Z.

Darleen whispered to herself, "One . . . two . . . three."

On three, Lucie raised her hand and said, "May I please be excused?"

"Oh, I am so surprised," whispered Darleen as Mr. Z gave Lucie the okay.

Kate and Lucie met in the girls' bathroom.

"Quick! Before someone comes!" said Lucie.

"*Woofa-woof!*" they said together and gave each other high fives.

Two seconds later, the door opened. A fifth-grade girl walked in and almost tripped over two dogs.

One was shaggy and ginger-colored. The other was smooth and white with spots.

As the dogs slipped out the door, they saw the girl shake her head and heard her say, "No way. I did not just see two dogs in the bathroom. I did not!"

Teacher's Pets

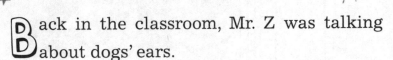

Back in the classroom, Mr. Z was talking about dogs' ears.

"When the ears are back, it may mean the dog is scared," he said.

Kate and Lucie slunk into the room with their ears back.

"When the ears are up, the dog is at attention," said Mr. Z.

Kate and Lucie stood tall and perked up their ears.

The class began to cheer.

Mr. Z had his back to the door and didn't know there were dogs in his room.

"I'm glad you're enjoying the lesson," he said to the class.

"Wow, Mr. Z! You brought in real dogs!" said Pete.

"You're the best substitute ever!" said Sara.

All the excitement made Mr. Z turn around. That's when he saw Kate and Lucie panting and wagging.

"Um, er, ah, well . . ." Mr. Z didn't know what to say.

Then the kids began to clap.

"Yay, Mr. Z!" they called.

"Thank you, thank you," said Mr. Z. "I should take a bow. I mean a bow-wow! Har-har-har."

Kate and Lucie waited to hear what Mr. Z would say next.

"When dogs are nervous, they often yawn," said Mr. Z.

Kate and Lucie showed the class how it was done.

"When dogs are happy and excited, they sometimes sneeze," said Mr. Z.

Kate and Lucie sneezed happily.

"These dogs are really smart," said Julia.

"They are totally cute, too," said Sara.

Kids started running up to pet the dogs. When Kate and Lucie saw the whole class coming at them, they slunk down and tucked their tails between their legs.

"Look, you're scaring them!" said Darleen. She stood up and said, "Class, sit!"

Something about the serious way she said it and the way her face looked made the kids run back to their seats.

Darleen turned to Kate and Lucie and said gently, "You're okay now."

Kate and Lucie went to Darleen and nuzzled their noses into her hands.

"Good dogs," said Darleen, petting them.

"You really know how to handle dogs," Mr. Z said to Darleen.

"I have two dogs," said Darleen. "I also have three cats, four hamsters, five fish, and—"

Just then the bell rang. Kate and Lucie made a run for it.

"To the tunnel!" whispered Lucie.

The dogs ran out to the yard and into the crawl tunnel. They said *"Woofa-woof!"* and tapped their paws together.

Woofa-wow! By the time the rest of the kids came out, Kate and Lucie were girls again.

"Did you see the dogs?" said Ben.

"Dogs? What dogs?" said Kate.

"The dogs that were in our class!" said Sara.

"There were dogs in class?" said Lucie.

"Oh right, you weren't in the room," said Julia.

"You missed everything!" said Pete.

The kids all started talking at once. More kids were coming from other classes.

Kate and Lucie went out the gate with smiles on their faces and their dog-bone necklaces twinkling in the sun.

Two Dogs, Three Cats . . .

"That was really fun!" said Kate, as the girls walked home.

"Yeah, Mr. Z is cool," said Lucie.

Up ahead a shiny blond ponytail caught their eye.

"It's Darleen," said Kate.

"You know, she was really nice to us when we were dogs," said Lucie. "Should we say hello?"

"Sure, why not?" said Kate.

They ran and caught up with her.

"Hi," said Lucie. "We hear you have dogs."

"And cats and birds," said Kate. "And frogs and—"

"I don't have any frogs," said Darleen. "But I do have two dogs, three cats, four hamsters, five fish, and one parrot."

"Wow!" said Kate and Lucie.

"We don't have even one pet," said Lucie.

"We both really, really want a dog, but we can't have one," said Kate.

"Why? Don't your moms like dogs?" said Darleen.

"They love them. But dogs aren't allowed where we live," said Kate.

The girls came to Kate's and Lucie's apartments. Their moms were out front, trimming bushes.

"Hi, girls!" called Mrs. Farber.

"How was school?" called Mrs. Lopez.

"You two live next door to each other?"

said Darleen. "No wonder you're stuck like glue."

"That's not very nice," said Kate.

"Why do you say mean things to us?" said Lucie.

"Well, you're always talking to each other," said Darleen.

"What's the matter with that?" asked Kate.

"Nothing, I guess. It's just that you never talk to me," said Darleen.

Kate and Lucie looked at each other. All at once they understood. Darleen acted mean because she felt left out.

"We're talking to you now," said Kate. "So can you stop being mean?"

"I guess so. Do you want to see my dogs?" said Darleen.

"Absolutely!" said Lucie.

"That would be really cool!" said Kate.

"Moms! We're going to Darleen's house!" they called.

"Have a good time!" called Kate's mom.

"Be home in time for dinner," said Lucie's mom.

The three girls went on to Darleen's house.

When they got there, Kate and Lucie got a big surprise.

Danny popped out of the house on the right. DJ popped out of the house on the left.

Kate and Lucie didn't know where to look first.

"Hi, guys," said Darleen.

"I can't believe it!" said Lucie. "You live next door to Danny and DJ?"

"Poor you," said Kate.

"They're okay," said Darleen.

"What are you two goofy girls doing here?" said Danny.

"We're meeting Darleen's dogs, for your information," said Lucie.

"Well, for your information, we're going to play basketball," said DJ.

As the boys walked off, the street filled with the smell of DJ's Banana-Fandana gum. It echoed with the sound of Danny's basketball. *Thunk, thunk, thunk.*

The girls heard scratching sounds at the door. They heard whining and saw tails wagging.

Two dogs were looking out. One was black. One was tan. One was really big, and the other was really little.

"They are so cute!" said Kate.

"What are their names?" said Lucie.

"The big black one's Bo. And the little tan one's Boo," said Darleen. "Come on, let's go in."

Kate and Lucie held out their hands for

the dogs to sniff. The dogs started wagging happily.

"They love being petted," said Darleen.

Kate scratched big Bo behind his ears.

Lucie sat on the floor, and little Boo jumped into her lap.

They heard a voice calling from upstairs.

"Hi, Darleen! Don't forget to feed the dogs."

"Okay, Dad. I'll do it right now," said Darleen.

"Ooh, can we help?" said Lucie.

"Sure," said Darleen.

First, the girls fed Bo and Boo. Then they fed the three cats, Whiskers, Fluff, and Mouse. Then the four hamsters, Eeny, Meenie, Miney, and Mo.

Then the five fish, Goldie, Fin, Swish, Glub, and Glitter.

"Hello, hello! Feed the birdie!" squawked the parrot.

"You're next, Ollie," said Darleen.

She filled his cup with seeds.

"Awk! Awk!" he said. "Ollie wants a ba-na-na!"

Kate and Lucie took turns giving him pieces of banana.

"Ready to walk Bo and Boo?" said Darleen.

"Ready!" said Kate.

"I'm so excited!" said Lucie.

Darleen laughed.

"I do it every day," she said.

She gave a leash to Lucie and one to Kate.

"Call them," said Darleen.

"Here, Bo!" said Kate.

Bo came running.

"Here, Boo!" called Lucie.

Boo came next.

Darleen helped put on the leashes, and they all went out.

"Hang on tight, Kate," said Darleen. "Bo pulls."

"I noticed that!" called Kate, who was already halfway down the block.

Lucie couldn't keep up with them because Boo was stopping to sniff every three steps.

After a while, Bo stopped running. Boo stopped sniffing.

Kate and Lucie got to walk the dogs all the way around the block.

They were in dog-walking heaven.

Homework Helpers

"Walking the dogs made me want to be a dog," said Lucie on the way home.

"Me too. Let's do it!" said Kate.

They were about to slip behind a big tree when . . . *Thunk, thunk, thunk.*

"Do you hear what I hear?" said Lucie.

"I hear it," said Kate. "Do you smell what I smell?"

"I smell it," said Lucie.

The scent of Banana-Fandana gum came floating their way.

The boys were bouncing and snapping down the street.

"Where are you two boys going now?" asked Kate.

"We went home for snacks," said DJ. "We're on our way back to the park."

"We have homework about animal communication," said Danny. "So we've got to go watch some animals."

"We already had that homework," said Lucie. "My report on pigeons got an A."

"My report on cats got one, too," said Kate. "Why don't you guys go look at some squirrels?"

"Maybe we will," said Danny. "Or we'll check out the dog run at the park."

Kate and Lucie elbowed each other.

"Dogs have very interesting body language," said Kate, trying not to laugh.

"A report on dogs could definitely get you an A," said Lucie.

"Yeah, well, whatever. See ya later," said Danny.

The boys started toward the park. Kate and Lucie quickly made a plan.

They slipped behind a hedge, came back out as dogs, and caught up with the boys.

"There are those dogs again," said DJ.

"We can study them, then go back to the basketball court," said Danny.

Kate howled. Lucie barked.

The boys took out their notebooks. They wrote, "*WOO-WOO!*" and "*RUFF!*"

Kate and Lucie knew DJ always had Chompy Chips in his backpack. They each pointed a paw back and forth between the backpack and their mouths.

"Wow, these dogs really know how to

communicate!" said Danny. "Give them some chips."

"I've got to write in my notebook first," said DJ. He wrote and read out loud: "Begging behavior. Point paws for treats."

DJ got some Chompy Chips from his backpack and tossed them to the dogs.

Kate and Lucie caught them in the air. They had to work hard to hold back their giggles.

For their next communication, Lucie wrote **BALL** in the dirt. Kate wrote **PLAY**.

"Amazing!" said Danny, grabbing his notebook. "I never knew dogs could spell."

"Wait till we give our report in class," said DJ, rolling the ball toward the dogs.

"We won't just get an A. We'll get an A++," said Danny.

The girls were proud. They had done their work well. They waved good-bye with their

tails. As they went, they saw Danny and DJ writing fast in their notebooks.

"I wish we could be there to see them give their reports," said Kate. "Do you think they'll get an A++?"

"I think they'll get A-goofy-goofy," said Lucie.

Cat Show Catastrophe

The girls had walked a few blocks when *sniff, sniff.*

"Do you smell what I smell?" said Kate, lifting her dog nose in the air.

"As in meow-meow?" said Lucie.

"Exactly," said Kate.

"Let's investigate," said Lucie.

The dogs followed their noses to the Tuckertown Community Center. Out front was a huge sign that said CAT SHOW TODAY.

As soon as Lucie saw the sign, she picked up speed.

"Where are you going?" said Kate.

"I smell cats, and I smell—"

Just then the side door of the center opened.

"Liver!" Lucie called over her shoulder.

Shimmy-shimmy-shimmy! Lucie's wagging tail put her backside into overdrive. She disappeared through the open door.

"Come back!" called Kate.

Too late. The door had already slammed shut.

Uh-oh, thought Kate. *I see trouble ahead.*

She pictured Lucie inside, surrounded by hundreds of cats.

I've got to get her out of there, Kate thought.

She stood guard at the door, waiting for someone to open it. While Kate waited, she listened. So far, she hadn't heard any people screaming. She hadn't heard any cats caterwauling. But with her shaggy, liver-loving friend inside, it wouldn't be long before there was chaos.

Finally, the door to the community center opened and Kate ran in. The room was filled with tables. The tables were filled with wire crates. The crates were filled with all kinds of cats, and all kinds of owners fussing over them.

"Here, Lucie, Lucie!" Kate whispered.

No answer.

She tried again. "Come out, come out, wherever you are!"

Kate heard rustling noises coming from behind a heavy red curtain. Then she heard crunching and snarfing-down-food noises. There was no mistaking who was making those sounds.

Kate peeked under the curtain. Lucie's head was buried inside a bag of liver treats.

"Do not take another bite!" hissed Kate. "You'll get sick."

"These are delicious," said Lucie. "Here, try one."

"This is not snack time," said Kate, joining Lucie behind the curtain. "We've got to change back to girls before anyone finds us."

"Oh, all right," Lucie said.

She gulped down the last treat.

Then Lucie held up her paw and said, "Ready . . . set—"

Kate and Lucie were about to say "Woofa-woof" and give each other high fives when the curtain jerked back.

"Eeeek!" screamed a lady from the cat show.

"Aaaaarf!" barked Kate and Lucie, jumping back.

"We're busted!" said Kate.

"Run!" said Lucie.

The cat-show lady hung on to the curtain, trying not to faint.

Kate ran left. Lucie ran right. They didn't realize they were going in opposite directions.

There were cats and people everywhere they looked. Ahead of her, Lucie saw a circle of Persian cats. She heard the judge saying, "Persian cats are elegant and calm."

"Reoowwww!" screeched the cats as Lucie raced by.

So much for calm, thought Lucie.

Meantime, Kate was passing a circle of Maine coon cats. The judge was saying, "Notice their long, beautiful coats."

Kate was noticing their long, beautiful coats standing on end and their backs arched high. The cats hissed and pulled at their leashes as she passed.

Lucie and Kate were darting back and forth, over and under grooming tables, in and out between show rings. People were screaming. Cats were caterwauling.

I knew this would happen, thought Kate.

Luckily, just as Kate reached the door, it opened.

Not so luckily, Lucie couldn't get to the door in time. She was being chased by a coon cat, who was being chased by her owner. They chased Lucie up a long flight of stairs.

Lucie ducked into a room. The room was a playroom for toddlers. There were no toddlers there now. Just lots and lots of toys.

I'll be safe in here, thought Lucie.

She used her back legs to push the door shut behind her. Then she looked up at the doorknob.

Uh-oh, she thought.

The big, round doorknob needed human

hands to open it. The only way Lucie could get human hands again was to have Kate beside her ready to work their dog-bone magic.

"A woo-woo!" Lucie heard a dog howling outside. She ran to the window and saw Kate running in circles, looking for her.

"I'm up here!" Lucie called.

Kate looked up.

"What are you doing there?" she called back.

"I got chased up the stairs," Lucie said.

"Well, come back down," said Kate.

"I can't. The door's closed, and I can't turn the knob," said Lucie.

"You've got to be kidding!" said Kate. "This is a catastrophe!"

"You mean a dog-astrophe," said Lucie.

"Har-har-har. Very funny," said Kate, rolling her eyes.

Just then, Lucie saw Carmen and George,

two workers from the local animal shelter, coming down the street. Someone must have called to report the dogs at the cat show. Their job was to rescue stray animals, and they were hurrying toward Kate.

"Run, Kate, run!" Lucie called from the window.

Kate didn't ask any questions. She just ran.

Carmen started chasing Kate. George looked up at Lucie in the window. The next thing Lucie knew, George was running into the community center.

Lucie heard footsteps coming up the stairs. She heard footsteps coming down the hall. She heard doors opening one by one.

The footsteps were getting closer. And closer.

They stopped outside the playroom.

Slowly, the doorknob turned.

The Getaway!

The door to the playroom opened. George looked around. He saw a play kitchen. He saw a book corner. He saw a block corner and a doll corner. Then his eyes passed over a corner of stuffed animals.

There were two teddy bears, a fuzzy owl, a ginger-colored dog with a big, floppy hat, a tall giraffe with a green leaf in its mouth, and a monkey holding a toy banana.

George scratched his head.

"Where's that dog I saw?" he wondered. "I must be in the wrong room."

He ran out and kept going down the hall.

When the sound of footsteps was gone, the ginger-colored dog jumped up and said, "Ta-daa!"

It was Lucie.

"Pretty neat trick, huh?" she said to the stuffed animals. "I saw it in a movie."

She shook the big, floppy hat off her head and headed for the playroom door. Thank goodness George had left it open when he ran out.

Lucie slipped out of the room and down the stairs. The cats had settled down, and the show was back to normal. As soon as the door to the center opened, Lucie ran out.

She was just in time to see Kate coming her way. Kate was panting, and her tongue was hanging out the side of her mouth.

"Hurry! Carmen is really fast!" said Kate.

"We're faster!" said Lucie. "Follow me!"

With Carmen closing in behind them, Lucie zigged. She zagged. She jumped over a planter. Then she turned a corner and ducked behind a bush. Kate was right beside her.

Carmen turned the corner at high speed and kept on going. She ran right past the bush where the dogs were hiding.

"Phew! That was a close call," said Kate.

"She might come back," said Lucie, trying to catch her breath. "We'd better change to girls fast."

"Woofa—pant-pant—woof!" they said and gave each other high fives. With a pop and a whoosh, they were girls again.

Kate and Lucie peeked out from the bush.

Carmen was coming back. And George was with her.

"We lost them," Carmen said to George.

"I hope those dogs will be safe and find their way home," he said.

"Thanks, George," Kate whispered to Lucie.

"We think we can find our way home," Lucie whispered back.

With Carmen and George out of sight, the girls came out from under the bush. On their way home, they passed the library and saw someone running up the steps. It was a familiar someone.

"Hey, look," said Lucie. "It's Mr. Z."

"Maybe he needs to read about animal communication for school tomorrow," said Kate.

A few seconds later, Darleen came

running down the library steps with a stack of books.

"Hi, Kate. Hi, Lucie," said Darleen. "I just saw Mr. Z going into the library."

"We did, too. Maybe he's going to do his homework," said Lucie.

"I'm going home to feed my pets," said Darleen.

"You're so lucky," said Lucie.

"Hey, want to come over and hang out with us on Saturday?" said Kate.

"Sounds good," said Darleen, waving good-bye.

Kate and Lucie kept walking toward home. A few doors up from the library was a dentist's office. They were surprised to see Mr. Z coming out.

"Wow, he did his homework already?" said Lucie.

"And got his teeth fixed, too?" said Kate.

"He's fast," said Lucie.

"So's his dentist," said Kate.

When the girls were almost home, they decided to go to Lucie's house.

"Hi, Mom!" called Lucie.

"Hi! We're in here," called Mrs. Lopez.

Both moms were in the bedroom trying on clothes for their blind dates. There were six outfits set out on the bed.

"I like that one," said Kate to her mom, pointing to black pants and a light blue top.

"I like this one," said Lucie to her mom, pointing to a flowered dress.

"Thank goodness you two came home," said Mrs. Lopez.

"We were stuck. We would have been here for hours deciding," said Mrs. Farber.

Then she started sneezing. "Ah-ah-ah-choo!"

"Are you okay, Mom?" said Kate.

"Ah-choo! Ah-ah-choo!"

Mrs. Farber couldn't even answer. Her allergies had kicked in.

"Have you girls been petting a cat?" said Mrs. Lopez.

"No!" the girls answered together.

They were glad they weren't telling a lie. They had been around lots of cats. And they should have remembered to clean off the cat hair. But they didn't pet any. How could they? They had been dogs. They'd learned their lesson when Lucie tried to pet Tiger.

Mrs. Farber was blowing her nose when Mrs. Lopez said, "We've got to go, Christy. We need to get to Fast Snips for our haircuts."

"Maybe some fresh air—*ah-ah-choo!*—will help," said Mrs. Farber.

"I bet it will," said Kate.

After the moms left, Kate said, "I'm going

home. I'd better get out of these cat-hair clothes before my mom gets back."

"Don't forget to take a shower," said Lucie.

"Meow!" Kate called over her shoulder, as she ran out the door.

Double Date

On Saturday, Darleen was at Kate and Lucie's, jumping rope outside. The three girls were making up Mr. Z jump-rope rhymes.

Har-har-har! Jump in my car.
I'll drive you fast, I'll drive you far.
How many miles will we go?
One, two, three . . .

Kate and Darleen were turning the rope and counting while Lucie jumped.

Then it was Darleen's turn to jump. They began rhyming again.

"Har-har-har . . ."

"You're the goofiest girls by far!" came a boy's voice.

It came along with the smell of Banana-Fandana gum. Of course. It was DJ.

Thunk, thunk, thunk. Danny was there, too.

Darleen tripped on the rope.

"You made me miss!" she said.

"Speaking of cars, who's pulling up at our curb?" said Kate.

The car windows were tinted, and the kids couldn't see in.

Then the doors opened. Mr. Z got out of the driver's side. Mr. Z got out of the passenger's side.

What was going on?

"Huh?" said all five kids together.

There were two Mr. Zs!

Their mustaches were trimmed and tamed. They had on cool suits and shiny shoes.

One Mr. Z said hi to Kate, Lucie, and Darleen. The other Mr. Z said hi to Danny and DJ.

At first, the kids were tongue-tied. All they could do was stare.

Then Kate said, "Oh my gosh, we really did have the same substitutes."

"Well, sort of. They're twins," said DJ.

"I noticed," said Lucie.

"That's how Mr. Z got from the library to the dentist so fast," Kate said to Lucie. "It wasn't one Mr. Z—it was two."

"What are they doing here?" said Darleen.

One Mr. Z walked up to Kate's door.

The other Mr. Z walked up to Lucie's door.

"I can't believe it! They must be the blind dates!" said Lucie.

"Believe it!" said Kate. "They're ringing our doorbells."

A minute later, the two Mr. Zs and the two moms were walking to the car. The moms were wearing the outfits the girls had picked. And their new haircuts looked great.

"Call if you need anything," said Lucie's mom to the girls.

"Be good," said Kate's mom.

"We'll see you later," said one Mr. Z.

"Don't get eaten by a gator," said the other.

"Later! Gator! That rhymes!" both Mr. Zs said together. "Har-har-har!"

The moms laughed, too. Then they all got in the car and drove off.

"Remember we said the blind dates might be goofy?" Kate said to Lucie.

"And our moms said they might be nice?" said Lucie.

"It looks like all four of us were right," said Kate.

"That was amazing," said Danny.

"You said it!" said Darleen. "What could be more fun than two Mr. Zs!"

Kate and Lucie looked at each other with woofs in their eyes. They knew what could be more fun. All they needed was a reason to slip away.

"Want to play hide-and-seek?" said Kate, grinning.

Quickly the kids did a counting-out rhyme. Danny was it.

He put his head against a lamppost and started counting.

Everyone else ran to hide.

DJ hid behind a tree. Darleen hid behind a mailbox.

Kate and Lucie ran off to the back yard.

"*Woofa-woof!*" they said together as they gave each other high fives.

Then they heard Danny call, "Ready or not, here I come!"

Danny found DJ. He found Darleen.

"Where are those goofy girls?" Danny said.

Just then, two dogs came out from the back yard. One had long ginger-colored fur. The other was mostly white with tan spots. Both dogs had silver collars with pink dog bones hanging down.

"It's showtime!" whispered Kate.

"Let's do it!" Lucie whispered back.

The two dogs stood on their hind legs and began to dance. Hop. Twirl. Dip. Roll over!

"I can't believe it," said Danny.

"It's those dogs again," said DJ.

"My dogs can't do that," said Darleen.

Hop. Twirl. Dip. Roll over! Hop. Twirl. Dip. Roll over!

"Ready for the grand finale?" whispered Kate.

"Ready!" whispered Lucie.

They turned around and put their tails together to make a big heart.

"How's that for animal communication?" whispered Kate.

"It's A++!" whispered Lucie.

The dogs took a quick bow, then ran behind the house.

Woofa-wow! They changed back to girls.

When they came out again, there were big smiles on their faces, and their pink dog-bone necklaces were twinkling in the sun.

THE END

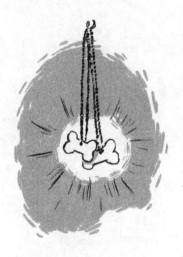

  If you love dogs,
raise your paw
and turn the page.

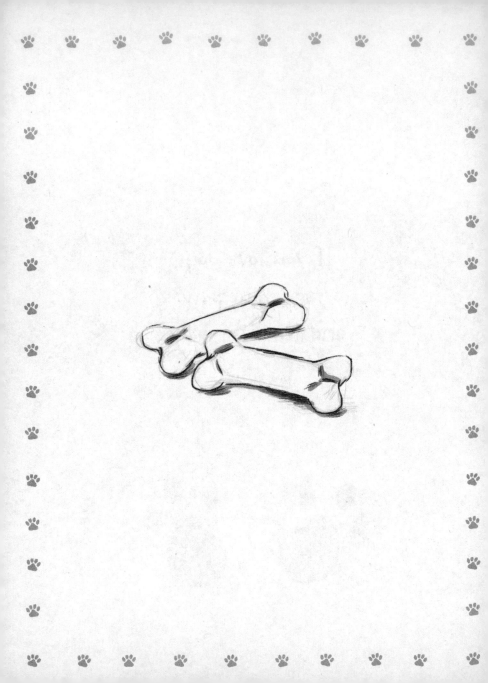

Woof-Ha-Ha!
Dog Funnies

Teacher: "Sam, what is the outside of a tree called?"

Sam: "I don't know."

Teacher: "Bark, Sam, bark."

Sam: "Bow, wow, wow!"

What did the dog do when he got 100 on his spelling test?

He took a bow-wow.

Why did the boy think his dog was great at math?

When he asked his dog what six minus six was, the dog said nothing.

What dogs can teach kids how to tell time?
  Watchdogs!

What kinds of stories do dogs like best?
  Furry-tales.

Which dog starred in the class comedy show?
  The Chihua-ha-ha!

Is Your Reading Teacher a Dog?

Did you know that in some schools kids read out loud to dogs? Special friendly dogs are brought into the schools, where they sit quietly and listen to children read. Some kids feel shy reading to teachers and classmates. But they enjoy reading to a dog.

That's because dogs don't tell kids they made a mistake. They don't tell them to speak louder. The dogs do cuddle up and listen. And sometimes they even give a reward—a lick on the nose. Best of all, having dog teachers really works. The kids become much better readers!

My Dog's Smile

By Stephanie Calmenson

Sketch by Stephanie

I wish I'd had my dachshund, Harry, when I was teaching in Brooklyn, New York. He would have been the perfect class visitor for a lesson on animal communication.

When I first met Harry, his body told a sad story. His eyes were dull. He kept his head down low and his tail tucked between his legs most of the time. That's because he had been an unwanted puppy living in a cage for too long.

It took some time, but with lots of love from everyone he met, Harry finally started to become a happy dog. His eyes brightened. His tail came up. He starting walking tall . . . well, as tall as a dachshund can be.

Then he made two special friends—a woman named Carmen Gonzalez and her snowy white poodle, Jeeter. The four of us starting walking together often.

One day, Carmen and Jeeter were coming down the street and Carmen called, "Haaaarrrrry!" Harry was so excited to see his friends that he did something very few dogs can do. He smiled like a person! His top lip went up, showing his shiny white teeth, and his eyes and nose crinkled.

The kids in my class would have laughed and laughed to see a little dog who could smile. When Harry smiles, he makes everyone around him happy.

Wacky Teachers, Wacky Dog

By Joanna Cole

Sketch by Joanna

It was fun to write this book because it's about dogs and school. I always liked school when I was a kid, and I was once an elementary-school teacher. But I wasn't wacky like Mr. Z. I've written about another teacher, Ms. Frizzle. I wasn't much like her either.

My little dog Taffy was kind of wacky, though. Once she climbed a tree! Here's how it happened. Outside our house, there was a tree with low-growing branches. Taffy was chasing a squirrel. It scampered up the tree, and so did Taffy. She just climbed up the branches as if they were steps. All our neighbors came out, and everyone laughed. No one had ever seen a dog climb a tree before!

Taffy was a Yorkshire terrier. You'll often see pictures of little Yorkies sitting in baskets with ribbons on top of their heads. They look so cute and innocent, but Yorkies were originally bred to catch rats. They are very fast hunters.

Once, on an island in Maine, I was walking Taffy on a leash down a dirt road. All of a sudden, I felt a little jerk on the leash. I looked down, and Taffy had caught a garter snake. It happened so fast, I hadn't even seen it.

Taffy was just one of the five dogs I have had in my life, but she was definitely the wackiest.

GOFISH

QUESTIONS FOR THE AUTHOR

Stephanie Calmenson

© Carlos Chiossone

What did you want to be when you grew up?
A kindergarten teacher.

What is the first story you had published?
"Buffy's Wink" was published in *Humpty Dumpty's Magazine for Little Children*. It was based on the time my favorite toy puppy had to get clean in a washing machine.

What's your most embarrassing childhood memory?
Fortunately, I've forgotten.

What's your favorite childhood memory?
Walking my neighbors' dog near the beach on summer mornings. The family liked to sleep late, so they left their door open for me. I'd slip in to get Lucky, their schnauzer, and off we'd go.

As a young person, who did you look up to most?
My uncle Eli was quite tall, so I'd have to bend my head way back. . . .

What was your favorite memory of school?
Every Friday afternoon, my fourth-grade teacher, Mrs. Riley, read aloud to us—everything from *Pippi Longstocking* to *Romeo and Juliet.*

What are your hobbies?
I'd say that writing is both my work and my hobby because I'd write even if I didn't get paid.

What was your first job?
In our late teens, my friend Karen and I ran a summer program for preschoolers and had so much fun. Our love of working with young children carried over into adulthood. Karen became a preschool teacher. I taught kindergarten, and most of the books I've written are for young children.

What sparked your imagination for the Ready, Set, Dogs! series?
Joanna and I were trying to come up with an idea that would be fun to work on together. Since we're good friends who both love dogs, we wanted to put friendship and dogs in our story. One day we were talking about growing up as dogless kids, and then knew we had to write about kids like us—kids who want a dog more than anything but can't have one.

If you could be any dog, what kind would you be?
Any poodle mix. No, wait, a Lab. Hold on, a dachshund! Ooh, ooh—a basset hound! Hmm, maybe a Great Dane . . .

Did you ever pretend you were a dog when you were little?
I did! A shaggy mixed breed. (See below for shaggy.)

Do you have any dogs?
My first dog was Rosie, who was sweet and shaggy and became a Visiting Dog, cheering up people in hospitals, nursing homes, and special schools. I wrote about her in *Rosie, A Visiting Dog's Story.* My dog Harry, who's beside me as I write, is a long-haired, chocolate-dappled dachshund. He's the star of *May I Pet Your Dog?: The How-to Guide for KIDS Meeting DOGS (and DOGS Meeting KIDS).* My dogs are great company and great inspiration.

What challenges do you face in the writing process, and how do you overcome them?
Sometimes I'll get an idea but am not sure how to turn it into a book. So I'll start writing, and if one approach doesn't work, I'll try another. And another. And another. If I'm still stuck, it's time to walk the dog.

Which of your characters is most like you?
Lucie and I have a lot in common. (Now, how did that happen?!) Like Lucie, I couldn't have a real dog, but I had lots of stuffed

dogs. When I was Lucie's age, I had long bangs that hung down into my eyes. And, like Lucie, I love to read about dogs.

What makes you laugh out loud?
When my dog Harry smiles at my friend Carmen. It happens if she talks to him in a wacky voice. His top lip goes up, which makes his nose scrunch up, and it's the funniest thing in the world.

If you could live in any fictional world, what would it be?
I'd live in the Swiss Alps with Heidi, Grandfather, Peter, his grandmother, and the goats. Of course, I'd have a few dogs.

What was your favorite book when you were a kid?
You guessed it—*Heidi*.

What book is on your nightstand now?
I'm rereading J. M. Barrie's *Peter Pan*. Naturally, I love that the children are watched over by "a prim Newfoundland dog, called Nana, who had belonged to no one in particular until the Darlings engaged her."

What is your favorite word?
Serendipity.

What's your idea of fun?
Walking a dog. My dog. My neighbor's dog. Any dog. I love to walk a dog.

If you could travel in time, where would you go and what would you do?
I'd go back to Rockaway summers, where I'd ride my bike, fly my kite, walk Lucky the schnauzer, float in the ocean, and make castles in the sand.

Do you ever get writer's block? What do you do to get back on track?
I don't worry about writing for *work*. I just write for *fun*—about anything from dogs to doughnuts. Of course, being a children's book writer, I often turn those ideas into books. So much for writer's block!

What do you wish you could do better?
Sing.

What would your readers be most surprised to learn about you?
Growing up, I was afraid to write and never in a million years thought I'd end up making my living as a writer.

What do you want readers to remember about your books?
The thing I'd like readers to remember about my books is they *enjoyed* reading them.

GOFISH

QUESTIONS FOR THE AUTHOR

Joanna Cole

© Annabelle Helms

What did you want to be when you grew up?
I never had the slightest idea what I wanted to be. It was just pure luck that I ended up being a writer.

What was your favorite thing about school?
I loved science class, writing school reports, and reading science books from the library.

When did you realize you wanted to be a writer?
I had always loved to write, but I never imagined that an ordinary person like me could be a real writer. Then when I was a young adult, I got a job at a news magazine answering the letters to the editor. I saw a lot of people like me who were writing for a living, and I realized that I *could* be a writer.

I asked myself, What should I write? The answer came easily. I would write what I had loved as a kid: science books for children. Later I branched out and wrote humorous story-books as well.

What sparked your imagination for the Ready, Set, Dogs! series?
I always wanted a dog when I was a child, but my parents said, "No, no, no." I had a goldfish, a turtle, a parakeet, and two cats. But never a dog. So writing about girls who couldn't get a dog was natural for me.

How did you and Stephanie decide to write a series together?
Stephanie and I have been friends for a long time, and we've written books together. We often say to each other, "How about this idea?" "How about that idea?" When we thought of writing about girls who wanted dogs, we knew it was the right idea!

What's your favorite childhood memory?
Making a garden with my aunt and uncle.

What are your hobbies?
Reading and writing.

What was your first job, and what was your "worst" job?
I had a job washing out test tubes in a health department lab. I liked it quite well. Another time I worked the night shift on an

assembly line making TV sets. I was very bad at it. I couldn't work fast enough, and things were always piling up behind me and slowing everyone else down. One night the foreman came over and said, "Honey, this isn't really working out for you, is it?" Wow! Was I glad to hand in my tools and get out of there.

What book is on your nightstand now?
I've just finished a wonderful novel for middle graders, *Counting by 7s,* by Holly Goldberg Sloan.

Where do you write your books?
I once lived in a house that had a built-in desk facing a beautiful view of a brook running through the woods. People would come over and say, "Oh, this must be where you write!" No way! When I write, I don't look around. I look at the computer screen. So I write in the attic, which doesn't have a view at all.

Did you ever pretend you were a dog when you were little?
No, but I did pretend to be a horse. Actually, I pretended I was the horse and the rider at the same time. For a while, I took a piece of rope to school and hung it under my coat. At the end of the day, I would "ride" home using the rope as reins.

Do you have any dogs?
I have had five dogs in my life: Taffy, Muffy, Harley, Suki, and Tater. I also like guinea pigs as pets. Once I had eight of them at

the same time. Most recently I had two named Chuck and Wee Chuck. Sadly, they got very old and finally died. Now I have two new ones: Pepper and Paprika. They are adorable, of course.

Which of your characters is most like you?
There are two characters like me. First is Arnold in The Magic School Bus. That's because, like him, I am not adventurous; I like to stay home and do quiet things.

The other is Ms. Frizzle. I'm not wacky like her, but I do like to explain science. That's not surprising, since that's what I do most of the time in my writing.

What makes you laugh out loud?
My husband, Phil, says funny things all the time. It's one of the reasons I married him. Another is that he likes dogs.

What do you do on a rainy day?
Get out my umbrella!

What's your idea of fun?
Playing with my grandchildren. (But when I get tired and want to take a break, they do not think I am any fun at all.)

What is your favorite word?
Chocolate.

Who is your favorite fictional character?
Anne of Green Gables.

Do you ever get writer's block? What do you do to get back on track?

I often get scared to write, especially when I come to a point where I don't know exactly what to write next. Then I'll avoid going to my desk. It's awful.

However, a few years ago, a friend gave me a tip that works for me: instead of starting to write in the usual way, tell yourself that you will work just for ten minutes. After that, you *must* stop. The next day, work for fifteen minutes. And so on. After a while, you find yourself back in the swing of things.

What's the best advice you've ever had?

The ten-minute trick.

What do you wish you'd known when you were younger?

The ten-minute trick!

When a friend's beloved pets go missing, Kate and Lucie are the girls—and the dogs!—to solve the mystery.

Ready, Set, Dogs!

Hot Diggity Dogs

Stephanie Calmenson & Joanna Cole

Illustrated by Heather Ross

They can't have dogs . . .   but they can be dogs!

Keep reading for
a sneak peek!

Summer Sizzles

Two dogs were trotting side by side down the street. They both had collars with pink dog bones hanging down.

One dog was mostly white with tan spots, tan patches around her eyes, and dark brown ears.

The other dog was shaggy, with ginger-colored fur that hung down almost to her eyes.

The dogs' tongues were hanging way out the sides of their mouths. They were both hot, hot, hot.

As they passed Didi's Bakery, they heard a voice booming from the radio. The voice belonged to Amos-on-the-Airwaves. He was Tuckertown's favorite radio personality.

"Grab your ice cubes, listeners! It's going to be a sizzling summer day!" said Amos.

"I'd love an ice cube right now," said the white-spotted dog.

"Make mine chicken-flavored!" said the shaggy ginger-colored one.

The dogs weren't yipping or barking. They were talking in words. That's because these were no ordinary dogs.

The dogs kept walking. The voice on the radio kept talking. This time the voice was coming from Bubble-Up Wash & Dry. Everyone in town listened to Amos-on-the-Airwaves.

"Remember, Bark-in-the-Park is coming soon," said Amos. "There'll be woofs, wags, and goody bags!"

The dogs stopped short. They looked at each other.

"Did he say goody bags?" said the spotted dog.

"He did," said the shaggy one. "Do you think they'll be for the dogs or for the kids?"

"It doesn't matter to us," said the first dog. "We can be either."

The dogs were just coming up to the Lucky Find Thrift Shop.

"Want to go in and look around?" said the spotted dog.

"Sure!" said the shaggy one. "But we know the rule."

A big sign in the window said NO DOGS ALLOWED. The dogs knew what they had to do.

"Let's go around to the back," said the spotted dog.

They trotted behind the shop. A minute

later, two girls were standing where the dogs had been.

One girl was Kate Farber. She had freckles that were like the white dog's tan spots. She was wearing glasses that looked a lot like the patches around the dog's eyes. Her dark brown pigtails looked like the dog's ears.

The other girl was Lucie Lopez. She had ginger-colored hair with bangs that almost covered her eyes. Her hair looked a lot like the shaggy coat of the ginger-colored dog.

The girls were both wearing I ♥ DOGS T-shirts and matching necklaces with pink dog bones. Their necklaces were a lot like the dogs' collars.

Each girl wanted a real dog of her own but couldn't have one. The girls lived next door to each other in garden apartments that had the same rule as the thrift shop: NO DOGS ALLOWED. But something amazing had happened. Instead of *having* dogs, Kate and Lucie had found a way to *be* dogs.

It had happened one day right in the Lucky Find Thrift Shop. The girls found two great-looking necklaces with pink dog bones and went into the dressing room to try them on.

They helped each other with the clasps and turned to admire themselves.

"These look great on us!" said Lucie.

"Let's buy them!" said Kate.

"*Woofa-woof!*" they said together, and gave each other high fives.

Woofa-wow! Just as their hands touched, the necklaces lit up. There was a pop and a whoosh in the dressing room, and two dogs were staring back at them from the mirror. The girls had turned into dogs!

After a few tries, they learned how to change back and forth whenever they wanted to.

Now that they were girls again, Kate and Lucie walked to the front door of the Lucky Find.

"I saw a big box of hats delivered the other day," said Lucie. "There were even some with pink ribbons!"

"Uh-oh," said Kate, rolling her eyes. "You and ribbons are a dangerous combination."

Lucie loved ribbons and everything pink.

"Hi, Mrs. Bingly!" Kate called to the store's owner as they walked inside.

Lucie took a quick look around the shop.

"Where are the new hats with ribbons?" she asked.

"They sold really fast," said Mrs. Bingly. "Everyone loved them."

"I did, too," said Lucie, looking disappointed.

Then she saw a basket of mini stuffed dogs.

"Look how cute these are!" she said. "I like the pink one best."

Since Kate and Lucie couldn't have real dogs, they had dog pj's and slippers, dog sheets and pillowcases, dog pictures, and even dog lamps.

Lucie's room was overflowing with stuffed dogs. She also had her own library of dog books. They were everywhere. She had read every one and knew a lot about dogs.

Kate's room was neat as a pin. All her things were carefully arranged. Her collection of little glass dogs was lined up in size order.

Kate was excited when she spotted a shelf with some glass dogs on it.

"I want one of those. I like the Yorkie," she said.

"You get that, and I'll get the pink dog," said Lucie.

"Wait, we have to see if we have enough

money," said Kate, being her sensible self.

The girls checked their pockets. Things at the thrift shop usually didn't cost much, and they were happy knowing the money they spent went to charity.

"I've got enough and money left over," said Lucie.

"Me too," said Kate.

"We're lucky dogs!" said Lucie.

The girls tried to keep straight faces as they went to pay Mrs. Bingly for their treasures.